KINSMOR

COURAGE IN THE SHADOWS

Scott Risch

The Journey of a Champion Book Four

TotalRecall Publications, Inc.
1103 Middlecreek
Friendswood, Texas 77546
281-992-3131 TEL
www.TotalRecallPress.com

ISBN: 978-1-64883-310-6
UPC: 6-43977-43106-6

Library of Congress Control Number: 2023934013

FIRST EDITION
1   2   3   4   5   6   7   8   9   10

This book is dedicated to my mother, whose mercy and compassion lead me to seek the personal God that she served.

About the Book

Kinsmor was a young shepherd boy who was taken by Roman solders and drafted into the Roman army.

During training in the Roman army, he became friends with Tallow, Grayboe, the doctor Luke, and was antagonized by Brutus.

Kinsmor quickly learned the skill of sward and shield. Over the years of training to be a soldier, Kinsmor gained strength and wisdom and became one of the Roman army's best.

Table of Contents

Chapter One: The Boy's Introduction...1

Chapter Two: The Boyhood Shaken...5

Chapter Three:...7

Chapter Four: A Friend's Face Emerges...9

Chapter Five: A Lesson from the Gladius 11

Chapter Six:...19

Chapter Seven:...25

Chapter Eight:...27

Chapter Nine: 30

Chapter Ten: 36

Chapter Eleven: The Conversation 41

Chapter Twelve: The Decision...44

Chapter One:
The Boy's Introduction

*****

The shepherd boy was daydreaming when he heard the "yelping" in the distance. He snapped out of his daze and walked toward the cries for help. The sheep would be fine, he wouldn't go far.

He arrived to see a mongrel dog cramped inside a rabbit trap. It half yelped and half growled in fear at the boy.

"It's okay boy." The kid said as he fed the dog fish scraps from his lunch. He then carefully raised the trap door, offering more fish at the bottom, as the dog sniffed and whined.

He fed his new friend from his hand as the dog winced away from the hand that was petting him.

"You can trust me, boy." The boy said compassionately.

"Kinsmor!" He heard his father in the distance.

He left the dog and grabbed his shepherd's staff.

*****

The bleating of the sheep greeted the man before the boy arrived. He tilted his head and looked around his son. "Who's your friend?"

Kinsmor was surprised as the wet nosed friend nuzzled his leg. "He was in a rabbit trap and he was hungry."

"I'll make a place by the sheep pin, but you'll have to get scraps from the market to feed him." His father stated.

Kinsmor knew what his father was saying. An extra animal meant extra food that they did not have. He would have to make this work somehow.

His made-up meal for that night was a loaf of bread and water. He knew he had to get something more solid.

Morning came and Kinsmor went to check on the dog. His father said to call it, "Willy", because he had doubts of "will he" make it as a pet.

The fresh turned dirt under the gate struck fear in Kinsmor's heart. He rushed to the gate and called. "Willy!" His fear swelled as his eyes filled with tears.

He heard a boy, with a rock filled hand, yell. "He went this way!"

Kinsmor followed the boy from a distance, fearing the worst. When he caught up with the boys, the worst was happening before his eyes.

The gang of boys had the dog trapped under a table, against a rock wall and were firing rocks from every side. All Kinsmor could do was cry at the helplessness of the dog.

All of a sudden, a screaming boy clutched his own hand as his rock tumbled at his feet. Two more grabbed their heads after being cracked with sticks from a boy with glaring eyes.

The head of this "gang" said "Get him!"

With that the boy bolted through the marketplace as rocks crashed behind him.

Kinsmor saw where the dog bolted and ran after him. He wouldn't forget the boy's actions, no matter who he was. He searched from the market to the surrounding edge of town for "Willy", but he couldn't find him anywhere.

Kinsmor cried himself to sleep that night, thinking of the boys and the dog, and not being there if it happened again.

*****

He woke to the sound of a dog playing with something. He burst through the back door to see his father jerking a rag with the dog on it.

"Look at the stranger that came to see us." His father spoke through his laughter.

He saw rocks in the hole that the dog made.

"I don't know how long that'll hold him. Just keep him fed in the pin and he'll know that's where his food comes from." His father said as Kinsmor hugged and pet the dog. Willy bathed the boy's face with his tongue.

Kinsmor tried to teach Willy to shepherd the flock, but he had no interest in it. The dog just wanted to play, now that someone loved him. The two grew closer as they spent more time with each other.

The boy grew stronger as he helped his father mend sheep fences and did the work of a shepherd. Willy kept getting out of his pin, but he'd always be home for dinner.

One night Willy didn't come home at all. Kinsmor saw his food undisturbed in the morning sun.

He'd asked his father and all he would say was that the wolves probably got him. "It was a long, cold winter and anything wild is probably starving."

Kinsmor thought that his father was probably right, but he put fresh food out anyway.

The sting of Willy's disappearance eventually left Kinsmor, but his contented life as a shepherd was not to be cherished for long.

Chapter Two:
The Boyhood Shaken

The meadow was peaceful as Kinsmor gazed at his flock. His daydream was interrupted by the clatter of weapons and the crack of whips.

He raced to the village as the cries of mournful mothers filled the air. He'd heard of this day, but it still came unexpectedly. Rome was taking boys to train as soldiers.

"Take the spindly boy. We can use him." A man from a wagon commanded.

"He's a shepherd!" A voice objected while grabbing Kinsmor's arm.

"So was King David of the Jews. Take him!" The same Centurion barked.

The boys were lined up and loaded into cage wagons where others with extended arms were knocked back with heavy soldiers' clubs.

Kinsmor's mother was held back by his father's loving arms. He saw her bury her face in his father's neck as the wagons pulled away.

He settled down and scanned the crowd that he was with. He recognized the leader of the gang and several of his "cronies", but chose to stay in the shadows just in case.

The wagon rocked along and most of its cargo was

asleep by the time they made camp that night.

The boys were kept in the wagons and food was given through the bars of the cage. Kinsmor saw the little hero in another wagon. He had gotten stockier, but Kinsmor recognized his face.

The meal consisted of some kind of mush, with little bits of meat sprinkled in it. He fingered through the mixture.

"I heard that it's …dog." A voice came from over his shoulder.

He snapped his head back to see a grinning face. "Listen. My dog was killed by wolves about a year ago. Your attempt to 'cheer me up' doesn't help." With that the boy sulked away and didn't say a word.

Kinsmor didn't like his own reaction to the boy, but his feelings for Willy were still raw in his mind. He thought that he'd better take down the stone fence if he wanted any friends. The only familiar friendly face that he had seen was in another wagon.

The wagon bounced along and everyone drifted back to sleep.

Chapter Three:
The Enemy's Face

The wagons reached their final destination and officers didn't waste any time barking out orders and slapping the boys into submission.

The boys were herded into the arena to meet Camp Prefect Marcus. "The time for mother is through. The time for father is through. From this time forward, Caesar is your mother, your father, your sister, and your brother. Your very life is Caesar's now. Your glory in the future is Caesar's."

He paused to let his words sink in. "Do you smell that, men?" He turned to the soldiers. "It smells like sweaty piglets." The men laughed. "Take these piglets down to the river and bathe them."

The boys were marched down to the river's edge and given the command to strip down to nothing because, "even your clothes are Caesar's". Their clothes were taken up and the blush of embarrassment covered most of the boys as they quickly entered the water. A few were water fearful, but a leather strap across their backsides helped them "overcome their fear".

Kinsmor found a secluded spot in the river to wash, while the others played and splashed. He went to a naked line, where boys took "Caesar's clothes", and went to get dressed.

"I see the mongrel's master made it to Rome."

He turned to see that the pudgy little boy from the market had turned into a mammoth.

He slapped Kinsmor's clothes to the ground and as he bent down to pick them up, he kicked dirt in his face.

When he laughed, a soldier named Darius stuffed a wad of grass and dirt in the boy's mouth. "How's the dirt, young Brutus?"

The whole line laughed as Brutus spat. Brutus wiped his mouth and glared at Darius.

Darius continued. "Some of you may think that you are 'lords' over the others. Remember, Caesar is your lord now. You are no one special." With that he kicked Brutus in the stomach, sending him to the ground, and walked off.

Kinsmor smirked at the sight of Brutus curled up on the ground, like a dying ant.

When everyone was back, they fell in line to get sandals for their feet. Kinsmor felt a sharp pinch on his shoulder muscles. He shrugged away from the pinch and turned.

"I don't care what 'Caesar' says. You will be my slave as long as we are here. You will get my meals and snap at my bidding. The soldiers can't always protect you." Brutus defiantly stated. He then grabbed the muscles again. "Kneel, slave!!" Kinsmor winced and fell to his knees.

So started Kinsmor's miserable days as a servant to his enemy.

Chapter Four:
A Friend's Face Emerges

Kinsmor saw the little hero in the distance. He looked like he needed a friendly face. He quickened his pace to catch up to the boy.

"Hello." He stated from beside him, while smiling.

The boy snapped his head in Kinsmor's direction. "What are you looking at?" Tallow blurted out.

A frown replaced his smile. "I was just being friendly!"

"Wait." Tallow pleaded.

Kinsmor turned with a scowl on his face.

"I'm sorry. Since the marketplace fight, I haven't had many friends. My name is 'Tallow'." He stuck his hand out with a reassuring smile.

"I knew about you before you put that big oaf on the ground holding his stones. My name is Kinsmor. The dog's name was 'Willy' and he'd gotten out of his pen that day. By the time I'd realized it, the boys were already chasing him down the street. I knew what they were going to do to him, but I was too afraid to stop them. There were so many times that I wanted to thank you, but I was too ashamed." With that, Kinsmor stuck out his own hand.

The grabbed each other's hand and began a fast friendship.

Tallow was curious so he had to ask. "You said, 'was'."

"What?" Kinsmor was surprised.

"You said the dog's name 'was' Willy. What happened to him?"

Kinsmor looked down. "The wolves got him last winter."

"I'm sorry." Tallow's apology was genuine.

As Kinsmor walked and talked with his new friend, their attention was drawn to the mob of boys around the Clarion board.

The boys parted for Tallow. Kinsmor stepped in front and snatched the paper from the board. His eyes scanned the paper. "It's the matches. Guess they've got you against. Brutus. The boy from the ma..."

"I know who he is." Tallow cut Kinsmor short.

Tallow studied the paper thoroughly. "It seems the fire is getting hotter." With that he handed Kinsmor the paper and walked away.

Kinsmor was dumbfounded. He didn't see anything on the paper about "fire", so he didn't have a clue of what his new friend meant.

Chapter Five:
A Lesson from the Gladius

He stepped into the arena and joined the other contestants awaiting "battle". Others spoke of their "combat" plans, but no one could predict how "plans" would change through hand-to-hand combat.

Tallow saw him from a distance and gave him a wink. Brutus saw him and gave him a "thumbs down".

When everyone had arrived, a familiar voice got their attention. "Alright you dogs of Caesar! The time for mother is gone. Forget her!"

Kinsmor's mind flashed to his mother's face buried in his father's neck.

The voice continued. "Caesar is your mother, your father, your sister and your brother. Your very life is Caesar's now. Your glory is Caesar's, so think of yourself as Caesar's."

The same voice got louder as it came closer to Tallow and Brutus.

"We will conduct a test of your skills with a gladius. It resembles the sword that you will one day use. We don't want you to kill each other before you've had the chance to die for Caesar.

Kinsmor saw Brutus jerk away as the man muttered something in his ear.

"Before the matches begin," He continued. "You will

practice three moves with each other. The upward block with the gladius," The man motioned a horizontal gladius above his head. "The slash block." The motion changed to the tip pointing up and sweeping to one side, and then the other. "And the downward block." The man portrayed a chopping motion with the gladius.

"Never stop a gladius with anything but another weapon. This is not only a good practice, it's easier than cleaning your blood off the weapon." A chuckle came from the men, but the boys were stone quiet. "Now you may begin." The man concluded.

The rattle of stone gladiuses filled the arena as boys mimicked their leader.

Kinsmor frantically blocked his opponent's blows with the examples that he had seen. He tried to fight back the panic and concentrate, but his opponent was fast and furious. He managed to block most of the blows with the gladius, until one dangerous blow came close to his face.

His eyes locked onto his hand wrapped around the stone. His opponent had a devilish grin and he stepped back to reveal the Centurion.

"Let me see your hand, boy." He said with a low growl.

"I said, LET ME SEE YOUR HAND, BOY!" The Centurion barked at Kinsmor's hesitance.

Kinsmor's hand trembled as he slowly brought it out in front of him.

The Centurion raised the stone gladius above his

head to chop Kinsmor's hand off. He flicked his wrist to expose the flat side on his hand. With one solid motion the stone came crushing down on Kinsmor's knuckles. The boy let out a scream that made even some of the seasoned soldier's grimace.

"Let this be a lesson to all of you." The Centurion continued. "We tell you these things not just for your learning sake, but also for your life's sake. Carry on."

Kinsmor insignificantly sleeked away, while everyone else's attention was drawn to their opponents.

When he found a place to be alone, Kinsmor unclenched his hand to look at the damage. Aside from the swelling, he could see a lump on the palm of his hand, on the reverse side of his knuckle.

"I know a man that can fix that for you, son." Darius said. "He's fixed worse things on seasoned soldiers."

Kinsmor stopped his sniffling and looked at Darius with pleading eyes.

"Let's go find Doctor Luke." He said as he clamped the boy's head in his forearm.

The two approached the man with a lamb curled in his arms. "Is that another rebel?" Darius said with a grin on his face.

"Yes. What brings you my way?" Luke said, looking at the boy.

"Young Kinsmor here got on the bad end of an officer's wrath." He nudged Kinsmor to show Luke his hand.

Luke tenderly took the boy's hand that trembled to

the touch.

"I'll be as gentle as possible." He grabbed the boy's wrist with his thumb and forefinger, and slowly looked at every angle of the hand. The lump was red and angry looking. He carefully set the hand down and started milling around in his shop.

"I've got some things to take care of." Darius looked as Luke waived him off.

"I'll bring him back when I'm done." Luke promised.

Kinsmor didn't know what to think about this. He was scared, his hand was in pain, and now he was alone with a stranger.

Luke pulled up the objects of his search. "Kinsmor, is it?"

The boy nervously nodded his head.

"I know that you're in a strange land, among people that you don't know, but I'd like you to know that I care about you."

The fear melted from Kinsmor's face. He understood what the man was saying.

"I'm going to be honest with you. You've got a bone out of place in your hand and the only way to get it back is to snap it back."

Kinsmor's smile changed to a solemn frown. He didn't like where this was going.

"I've got two flat boards to put your hand between. I've seen injuries like this before and, believe me, this is the only way to fix it." Luke said as he bowed his head.

As he raised his head Kinsmor gave him a pleading

look then swallowed hard. "Okay." His voice cracked.

Luke quickly and carefully adjusted the boy's hand between the boards. "Can you hand me the cup of water across from you?"

Kinsmor strained to reach and Luke stamped down on the board. The bone snapped back into place with a muffled "pop". Kinsmor's head and body twitched back, and he slowly curled his fingers back and forth to test his hand. He winced a little with each movement, but was relieved that he could move more.

"The movement will be sore at first. Take this stone and practice curling your fingers on it."

Kinsmor took the rock and carefully began wrapping it with his fingers. "Thank you, Sir."

"You can call me Luke. I want to be your friend, and the God I serve wants to be your friend as well. God knows how weak we are, that's why He extends his mercy to us."

"Sir, I don't know what you're saying. Which god wants to be my friend? My father worships the gods all the time. I've seen his alters in the garden." Kinsmor was genuinely dumbfounded.

Luke smiled at the boy's innocent perspective, but tried to break things down to his level. "When you got hurt, did Darius take you to a blacksmith for your injury?" He asked with a smile.

Kinsmor grinned and shook his head.

"He came to me because I know how some of the human body works."

"The God that I serve knows all about the human body and, more importantly, the human soul. He cares deeply about both."

"We, as humans, have always had a disease in our soul called sin sickness. It is something that we are born with."

"I don't understand about...'sin sickness'." Kinsmor was confused.

"Have you ever told a lie?" Luke asked as Kinsmor nodded his head in embarrassment. "Well, that is because mankind has a 'sin' nature. We as humans don't have a nature that does good things for God. The nature we have does things for ourselves. That's part of our 'sin nature'."

"The God of the universe wants to have a relationship with man that He created, that's why He sent His son, Jesus."

"Jesus promised that when we accept what He did on the cross as being for us, that He would give us part of his spirit. He would heal our sin sick souls." Luke looked at the confused boy before him.

"You act as if this god that you serve is the only god!" Kinsmor was confused and a little irritated that Luke hadn't mentioned any other god.

"I know that this is a lot to comprehend, but please leave thinking of this. The God that I serve loves you and only wants the best for you."

Kinsmor settled himself with Luke's words. "Sir, I appreciate your help with my hand, but give me time to think more on these things that you told me." He turned to walk out.

"Let me go with you." Luke asked.

"I know my way back." Kinsmor said defiantly.

"I told your captain that I would bring you back. You wouldn't want me to break my word, would you?" Luke smiled.

Kinsmor shook his head and thought that he was in for another round of "the god I serve". Luke left the boy alone and the two walked in silence for the short distance.

*****

The next morning Kinsmor was expected to go through his normal routine of things. His hand was "fixed", according to his superiors, so he was not excused from his duties as a soldier of Rome.

The afternoon brought smiles from his friend, Tallow. "I'm sorry about your hand. I'll try to help as much as possible. I guess you'll have to train your other side."

With that Kinsmor brought up a stone gladius inches from Tallow's face. It was stopped only by Tallow's gladius.

"You mean like that." Kinsmor had a devilish grin on his face.

They lowered their weapons and exchanged a comrade's hug.

"The 'physician' gave me this to keep my fingers busy and strengthen my grip." Kinsmor reached out and exposed the rock in his hand. He then told him of "Dr. Luke".

The two boys' friendship grew as they got older. Kinsmor was still antagonized by Brutus, the oaf from the village, but Tallow's friendship made things more bearable.

Chapter Six:
Kinsmor's First Battle

The man rose from the bunk he had entered as a child. The stone that his fingers once wrapped was now covered by his palm. Over the years training his stature had grown from a scrawny, little whelp to a strong, toned warrior. The Roman Army had made sure of that.

He still had questions for Luke, but learned of Rome's attitude toward Christians and kept them and his "meetings" to a minimum.

Today's events would be memorable for him and his friends. This would be their first real battle. They would no longer face straw mannequins that didn't fight back.

The Northern Army had pushed their way on to Caesar's lands and they had to be squelched again.

Kinsmor fell in line with the others and received a soldier's sword and shield. The weapon felt light in his hand compared to the stone gladius that he was used to holding. Several others were motioning the same manner as he. They were checking the "lightness" in action.

They marched for half a day's journey to a mountain side. They could hear the Northern Army's chants before they got into position.

The yells from both sides of the valley rang throughout the region.

The Northern Army was the first to "charge" as the fierce warriors ran toward each other. Kinsmor had seen Tallow jump and hit a mannequin with both feet, so he tried to do the same thing in this battle. As soon as he left his feet, his opponent stepped aside and let Kinsmor stumble on the ground.

Kinsmor rolled to his feet just as an axe buried in the ground where his head had been. His blade sliced through the man's hand and opened his belly with ease. Something told him to "Bend over!"

With his sword clenched between his hands, he thrust it through his legs and into a man's torso. With his hands still on the sword, he flipped over and got to his feet. The man's pleading eyes looked straight into Kinsmor's. He then took the sword and ripped it up to the man's chest.

Kinsmor saw other opponents running as the call came. "Stop! Do not pursue them!"

He shouted his victory with his battle mates until the hillside rumbled with their voices.

The foot soldiers were called back to the original mountainside. Marcus had a special task for the archers while the rest of the men kept the army busy.

Kinsmor waited as the archers left with Marcus. He was told to look for the "fire shot" in the sky.

It wasn't long before the Northern Army was on the offensive again. Warriors came at them with the same fierceness as before.

Kinsmor picked a javelin off the ground, just when a

warrior went airborne. He braced the pole between a rock and the ground. The soldier's face showed horror as the spear's point burst through the skin of his back. He crumbled at Kinsmor's feet and he pursued another.

Before long this "snake" of the Northern Army was slithering back into its hole. The "fire shot" in the sky told Kinsmor that relief was in sight.

This time they were allowed to pursue their attackers. The fierceness of the warriors died as they saw their friends' lifeless bodies on the ground.

Kinsmor's opponent saw the devastation and immediately dropped his weapon, shot his hands up and turned. His face was covered in horror at the carnage of the battle. He preceded Kinsmor before the tip of his sword. The face that was once fierce now showed fearful eyes that welled cowardice tears. He was lined up with the others and stood trembling.

"Who leads this rabble set before me now?" Marcus demanded. "What? No volunteers. You were so brave on the field with swords and shields. Did someone cut out your tongues?"

"Our officers...are dead, Sir." Kinsmor's captive shook.

Marcus went to where the voice was. The man was still trembling over a puddle that he had created.

"Why are you still alive? You should've laid down your own neck for your captain." With that Marcus ran his sword all the way through the man's trunk. The man's face gasped as his life slipped away. Marcus pulled his weapon from the quivering body while Kinsmor and the others backed away.

The sight of Marcus' kill made a memory more than Kinsmor's first kill.

After the rest of the army scampered over the hill, while being chased by arrows, Marcus gave the order. "Let's go home."

Kinsmor was relieved at the thought of home. His body was aching from the strains of war. He was wishing for the mannequins. Mannequins can't match your strength for strength. He placed his sword back in its sheath and stepped into the wagon.

*****

Kinsmor noticed a faint light in the halls as he walked through the garrison. He approached the light and found his friend in deep thought of the day's events. "I would've thought that you'd hit the sack early, considering how you fought today." His words fell dead in the air.

"Tallow, what's weighing so heavy on your brow?" He was worried.

"I spoke with one of the warriors before he died." Tallow said, still deep in thought.

"He was begging for mercy, no doubt." Kinsmor joked.

"It was quite the contrary. He asked me if I 'knew the one he was going to meet?' He had such a look of peace on his face."

"The gods must've been good to him." Kinsmor

reasoned.

"It wasn't the gods. He spoke of a man named…Jesus?" Tallow questioned.

"Oh. Ciaphus had that man, Jesus. He delivered him to Rome to kill, because the Jews didn't want to get their hands dirty." Kinsmor was a little irritated.

"He talked of being …forgiven." Tallow continued. "I asked him of whom did he need forgiveness? He said that he was forgiven by the Creator when he believed in Jesus as the Christ, the Messiah."

"Yes, I know of that Jew and all that he claimed. If you ask me, anyone that is affected by that man has been changed into a weakling."

Kinsmor received a slug from his friend and scowled at him.

"Some are weak before they even hear of the man." Tallow winked and grinned.

A sheepish grin spread across Kinsmor's face as he rubbed his shoulder. "Remember, you're a Roman soldier. You have no lord but Caesar. You don't need that Jew's religion." Kinsmor said, trying to discourage his friend.

"You recite our leaders well, but how do you feel about forgiveness? My friend, everyone needs forgiveness at some point in their life." Tallow admitted as he walked off.

Kinsmor did not like the direction his friend was leaning. His words reminded him of Luke from years ago. He still spoke with Luke from time to time, but this new thought of "forgiveness" from Tallow shocked him. Luke, he could discount and write off as "one of those" Jews. Tallow was his friend. He felt betrayed.

He didn't get much sleep that night.

Chapter Seven:
His Enemy

Kinsmor doused his head and face with cool water from the well. He was trying to wake himself from the sleepless night.

He turned his body and was confronted with an old nemesis.

He snapped his sword out against the mammoth before him. "Have you come to collect an old 'debt'!?"

Brutus stood with his hands raised in submission. "You have no 'debt' with me. My debt is to you."

"In our early years, I was a tyrant to anyone weaker and you bore the brunt of that."

"I was overseeing a village where a little servant girl was trying to befriend a mongrel dog. The beast had a nasty attitude that she was trying to get around."

"I asked why she didn't get a nicer animal to be her friend. She said, 'Someone taught this dog to be mean. I'll show him how to love.'"

Kinsmor was eager to hear the rest of the story, but his distrust of Brutus was all over him.

"I told you this story to let you realize how sorry I am for those early years. Would you take the hand of this 'mongrel dog' and forgive me for the early years?" Brutus eyes pleaded with his big hand extended.

Kinsmor was beside himself. This boy that once

made him bow under his iron fist was now a compassionate man asking his forgiveness. All the years of bitterness and anger had to be resolved. How could he give all that up, with no retribution?

His eyes welled up as forgiveness "bled" through. He grabbed Brutus' hand and embraced him hard as a new friend.

After the embrace Brutus talked of the battle. "I saw you open up that soldier's belly on the field. You're quite the tumbler."

Kinsmor's face blushed at the attention. "Thanks for the warning."

Brutus looked dumbfounded. "What warning?"

"You told me to 'bend over'." Kinsmor stated.

"I was too busy putting a spike through someone's back." Brutus argued.

"Someone told me to 'bend over' when we were on the field." Kinsmor continued.

"How did you hear it with all the clatter of battle?" Brutus laughed incredulously.

"Surprisingly they weren't yelling." Kinsmor said.

"If it was a still, small voice or impression, listen carefully. It was probably from somewhere other than the ground we share." Brutus spoke solemnly as he turned and walked off.

Chapter Eight:
More Questions for "The Physician"

Luke was busy writing on a parchment as Kinsmor watched from the doorframe. He was unaware of the eyes on his back.

He turned in Kinsmor's direction and his eyes lit up. "I see a warrior has grown from the hurt lamb of years gone by." He threw his arms around the man and Kinsmor smiled and did the same.

They broke the embrace and Luke pulled the once injured hand up. Kinsmor opened up the palm.

"I see that, not only did the stone change your hand but, your hand changed the stone." The stone was now "palm-smoothed" and gleamed in the sunlight.

"I'll bet that you thought I'd forgotten you." Kinsmor laughed.

"The thought had crossed my mind. I've been praying for you; that God would clear the confusion from your mind and make His message clear."

Kinsmor paused before he spoke. "That is what brings me your way." He then told Luke of the battlefield experience and Brutus' response to his questions.

Luke constrained himself as he spoke. He could see God's hand working, but wanted Him to lead. "Kinsmor. There is a special plan for you. That is why

God warned you on the battlefield. That is also why He healed your hand so wonderfully. God wants a relationship with you."

"You are a precious treasure to Him. Brutus was right. That 'voice' was from somewhere other than the ground we share."

Kinsmor listened to what Luke was saying. "You speak so highly of this 'healer' that you serve. You act as if you know him like a 'friend'. How is he different from all the other gods that are prevalent in Rome?" Kinsmor said with a little antagonism in his voice.

Luke resolved to handle Kinsmor carefully. "Well, the healer was my friend. I walked with Him daily. Jesus told us all about his death. We didn't want Him to go through it, but he gave us a promise. He said that even after he died, he would give us of his spirit; and not only us, but anyone."

"From that point I have had peace in my life. You can have this peace that I speak of. Jesus promised it to anyone who believes in Him."

Kinsmor could not fight the tears as they filled his eyes. Luke saw this and pressed on. "I see that you're still conflicted. Kinsmor. God wants a personal relationship with you. Please release whatever is holding you back, to Jesus, the Christ. You will find true peace when you do."

Kinsmor turned his face to the sky. "God, I don't know if what this man is saying is true, but he's truer than any other man I've seen in my life. If he is true, and he represents you, then you are truer than the gods I know."

"Forgive me for my blindness all of these years. Change my way of thinking to match his."

When he finished, he noticed Luke's eyes still shut while his lips moved in silent prayer. "Amen." Luke said audibly.

"Oh, is that how you do it?" Kinsmor asked.

Luke smiled. "I had a good teacher. I must warn you about Rome's view of the way you're thinking now. If you take Jesus as your King, it will go against Caesar being your king."

"I know what Rome thinks. That is what took me so long to decide. Don't worry. I'll choose my words carefully." Kinsmor firmly shook Luke's hand with a shoulder embrace as he walked away.

Chapter Nine:
A New Concept: Forgiveness

Kinsmor didn't know what to think about this new decision that he made. He definitely would have more conversations with Luke. While he thought on these things, a tap on his shoulder broke him from his concentration.

A dark headed man stood grinning at him. Kinsmor's countenance dropped at once. This was the one they called "Larimor" or "Liarmore". He always had something to stir up with the men. Whether it was true or false, you'd better think twice before you believed him.

"Kinsmor, is it?" Larimor acted innocent.

"Where's my sword?" A thought rushed in. "What do you want, Liarmore?" Kinsmor intentionally mispronounced.

"I have some information about Grayboe that you might find interesting." Larimor said while still grinning.

"Who is this 'Grayboe', and why would I be interested in him?" Kinsmor did not hide his frustration.

"You had a dog named Willy, right?" Larimor was almost giddy with this knowledge.

"Yes." Kinsmor was offended that anyone knew of

that, much more the 'gossip' of the garrison.

"Grayboe is the one that used him for archery practice." Larimor said.

"Where did you get that tale?" Kinsmor objected to his incredulous story.

"I overheard a conversation between Prefect Marcus and another officer. He said that it was a mongrel dog from your village. It could've been someone else's dog, but it was 'well cared for', as he put it." Larimor threw his hands up with innocence.

"Why don't you go bother someone else with 'interesting information'?" Kinsmor blew Larimor off.

Larimor went off with his back turned and waived a finger in the air, as if to say. *"You'll be sorry."*

*****

Kinsmor told Luke of the conversation and all that he knew about Larimor as an unreliable source.

"There is a proverb of King Solomon of old." Luke began. "It says that 'a man meddling in an argument not belonging to him is likened to a man taking a strange dog by the ears.' I am not going to 'take this strange dog by the ears'."

"You have the Spirit of God in you. He will give you the wisdom that you need." Luke patted Kinsmor's back to encourage him.

"If what he says is true, I'll need help with forgiveness." Kinsmor's realization was honest.

"Well, before you pursue this, talk to someone else that might know more than Larimor knows. Two people saying the same thing is better than one of questionable character."

Kinsmor was already nodding his head.

Luke paused to let Kinsmor think on what he said. "Jesus said that if we don't forgive men when they have wronged us, then our Father will not forgive us. The way that you have chosen is not just the way of forgiveness from the Father, but also forgiveness for men. Kinsmor, would you mind if I pray for you about this?"

He just nodded his head. "Pray."

"Father," Luke began. "This young man is new to surrendering to Jesus. I pray that you will bring truth to him on this matter, and that you will help him to pursue truth and forgiveness. I ask this in Jesus' name. Amen."

*****

Kinsmor stood at the doorframe and wondered what kind of "captain" he would be addressing.

The captain will see you now." A stern-faced soldier waved him on.

He nervously approached the room where Prefect Marcus sat.

"Come in." Marcus called before he saw Kinsmor.

"Prefect, Sir. The reason I wanted to see you is to check out a rumor that I've heard. Do you know an archer named Franci…uh…Grayboe?"

Prefect Marcus hadn't heard of 'Francis' in years. For that matter, he hadn't seen this kid in years. He had certainly gotten bolder than the shy child of years ago.

"I know the man. What is your concern with him?" Marcus was guarded.

"Do you know anything about him killing a dog years ago?" Kinsmor knew that he was "starting" something.

Marcus knew of the incident and he also knew that it would come back to bite him one day. His irritation came out in his speech. "You are a Roman soldier. Don't worry about a 'pet' that you had years ago. Vengeance is Caesar's, not yours. Leave me now. I've got more important things to worry about than a 'mongrel' dog!"

Kinsmor left disappointed, but at least Prefect Marcus confirmed Liarmor's story. Thoughts of forgiveness kept coming back in his mind. He knew less about Grayboe than he did about Prefect Marcus, but something told him to forgive Grayboe. That, according to Luke, was the Spirit of God.

*****

Kinsmor leaned his skinny frame against the doorpost.

"Can I help you?" Grayboe asked.

"You don't know me, do you?" Kinsmor asked.

"I've seen you with that Tallow fellow. What's your business here?" Grayboe's whole demeanor was barbed.

"I'm going to tell you a story that will explain my 'business' here, but first let me introduce myself." His tone was calm. "My name is Kinsmor."

"I grew up in the same village as Tallow. We didn't

know each other, but once I saw what he did for my dog I knew we'd be friends."

"'Willy', that was the dog's name, had gotten out of his pen. A group of boys chased to the east of the village. When I caught up to them, Willy was huddled under a small table and trying to back against the wall away from the shot of rocks the boys were throwing."

"This kid came from nowhere, cracking heads and hands with sticks before they realized what was on them."

"Tallow" Grayboe guessed.

"Yes. He led the boys out of town, while Willy bolted from his hiding spot. Willy showed up the next morning with a hole in his thigh that someone tried to bandage."

"Tallow" Grayboe said skeptically.

Kinsmor nodded his head in affirmation.

"I heard that he walloped ten of those brats that day." Grayboe laughed.

"It was only five." Kinsmor rolled his eyes. "Willy's leg mended and I enjoyed him for almost six months."

"One morning I came out and found that he had dug under the gate to get out. After looking everywhere, and crying many tears, I was at a loss. My father said that Willy went to the woods and the wolves got him."

"How did you know about me?" Grayboe was irritated.

"Let's just say that the grapevine branches to places that you don't know." Kinsmor remained calm.

"Look! If you came for an apology, I'm sorry. I really didn't think of that dog as 'belonging' to anyone. I'm sorry that I killed your 'pet'."

"I thank you for that, but that's not why I'm here. I came here to offer you…forgiveness." Kinsmor said compassionately.

"Wait a second." Grayboe was surprised. "You didn't know me, but you forgave me before we met."

"That's right." Kinsmor stated.

"Why?" Grayboe was incredulous.

"I realize that it sounds strange but, it is because I've been forgiven that I forgive." Kinsmor said as he smiled.

"I don't know you, but I have a question." Grayboe was suspecting the answer. "By whom did you need forgiveness?"

Kinsmor swallowed hard, knowing Rome's view of Christ's followers. "I've been forgiven by God."

Chapter Ten:
Kinsmor's Friend Returns

Kinsmor had heard that Tallow was back from his journey, so he was anxious to catch up with him. So many things had happened since he'd been away. As these thoughts bounced in Kinsmor's head the same friend called to him, "Kinsmor."

Tallow was sitting on Brutus' haunch, while his face was facing the dirt. Kinsmor wrapped his body around Brutus' leg while Tallow took a knife to the other. Brutus had a thorn in his calf that needed to be dug out. Kinsmor felt the big man twitch and squirm as Tallow's knife point went deeper.

Others had come to make sure the big man stayed down. They grabbed arms and limbs. Someone even grabbed Brutus' head. They were probably afraid that he would bite his way out of his predicament.

Brutus' body tensed up as Tallow dug deeper. "'Bout got it." Tallow stated.

Brutus let out a grunt and expelled gas.

"Let's hope the rabbit doesn't come out next." Tallow joked as Kinsmor and the men laughed. "I got it!" He shouted. "Give this man a drink and dress that leg."

Kinsmor went to work on the wound, which wasn't easy, as the big man thrashed around. He had just finished when Tallow grabbed Brutus' hand and they both hoisted him up.

Tallow spoke softly to Brutus and Kinsmor saw Brutus' face change like he'd seen a ghost. Kinsmor drilled his new friend with. "What did he say to you?"

Brutus held up his hand to stifle Kinsmor. Once he stopped the "rattle" of questions, he thought carefully before he spoke.

"Tallow has been through a lot, but now what the Senate is asking him to do is of a grave nature. I think that he could use his 'best friend's' ear. Go to him and listen. You'll learn more than any conversation that we have." Brutus swallowed the small man's shoulders with his arm.

Kinsmor was frustrated that Brutus stone walled him, but he could see the big man's point. He would try to get a moment alone with Tallow. With all the garrison wanting to see him, it would be hard.

*****

The evening meal was pleasant for everyone. Kinsmor saw Tallow beside the fire, finishing off a rib of the beast they had.

He rolled a stump next to his friend. "I know that you've had a lot on your mind and you're just settling back into things around here, but I have questions as one friend to another."

Tallow thought deeply about his relationship with Kinsmor. *Would their friendship be able to withstand what he had to tell him?* His thoughts were conflicting in his own mind. *How could he explain to someone else?* Kinsmor was a good friend, so he decided to trust him.

"When I left the first time, although it was on assignment, I still had questions that couldn't be answered militarily."

"Was it because of that dying soldier?" Kinsmor asked, with a gentle tone.

"Yes, it was." Tallow noticed a change in his friend. "I met a Jewish priest there named Nicodemus. He kept me from cutting off a bandit's hand in the marketplace. I told him that I had questions that he would be able to answer better than anyone I knew."

"Are you still inquiring about Jesus?" Kinsmor wasn't really surprised.

"I haven't made up my mind about him, but I've noticed that those who've had contact with him are changed to some degree." Tallow stated.

Kinsmor thought for a moment. "I've been talking to one of Jesus' disciples. Do you remember when my hand was injured years ago?" Kinsmor asked.

"You mean when the Centurion broke your hand." Tallow was still upset by the act.

"Well, my hand has recovered, and so has my spirit, because of Luke." Kinsmor said as he looked at his friend intensely.

"So, you're on a first name basis with him." Tallow tried to be skeptical.

"I observed the man as he spoke. I couldn't find any cross words from him, even when I doubted his God. He told me that I could have the same relationship with the God of the Universe." Kinsmor stated.

"Don't tell me that you're one of 'those' too!" Tallow objected.

Kinsmor was taken back. "What do you mean, 'one of those'?"

"One of those 'Christians' or 'little Christs' as I've heard!" Tallow was visibly upset.

"Tallow, don't worry, I'm still your friend. I just need to tell you what happened on the battlefield."

"Brutus let me know a little bit of your conversation, but fill me in on the rest." Tallow sounded eager.

"Well, I really thought Brutus told me to 'bend over' that day. He was the only one nearby. He denied it, saying he was busy in battle."

"I spoke to Luke about it and he said that God had special plans for me. One of the things that Brutus told me was that the 'voice' I heard probably came from somewhere 'other than the ground we share'."

Tallow thought for a moment. "Kinsmor, part of what I told Brutus was that the Senate wants to 'show off' my talents in the arena as a gladiator. The reason I tell you this is to ask you the same question my father asked me on my visit with him."

"'What if they toss Christians in the arena, as targets and lion food?'" Tallow looked with pleading eyes at his friend.

Kinsmor's face was struck by the harsh reality of Tallow's words.

"I know there's no changing you from this course."

Tallow continued. "I'm asking you as a true friend to keep this 'faith' as hidden as possible."

"I'm new to this 'faith', as you called it, as well. I'm of the opinion, also, that God will take care of me, if I trust Him with everything." Kinsmor said with a smile on his face.

Chapter Eleven:
The Conversation

~

Kinsmor's thoughts could not escape the conversation he had with Tallow. The sleepless night was evidence of that.

The thought of Rome hunting him down put him on edge. He knew that he had to talk with Luke to settle himself.

He approached Luke's stable to find him, not attending to a lamb or any other hurt beast but, but bent over in prayer. His prayer was so fervent that he didn't notice Kinsmor until he got close.

Luke's eyes scanned Kinsmor all the way to his face. "Hello, my friend. What is weighing so heavy on you today?"

"Is it that evident?" Kinsmor was surprised. He wanted to lead into this conversation softly.

"Are you worried about being thrown into the arena?" Luke had a sense of "knowing" about him.

"What have you heard?" Kinsmor panicked.

"I was thinking that with the 'games' coming, they would need soldiers to be available as target." Luke explained.

Kinsmor eased a little. "I am worried, but not because I'm a soldier of Rome. My friend Tallow told me that he thinks they might put...Christians in the arena." Luke finished the statement with Kinsmor.

"How did you know?" Kinsmor was shocked.

"I could call it an 'impression' but, really it was God telling me of the trouble that people of this 'faith' are in store for."

"I am comforted with this. Jesus said that he who will cling to this life, will lose it, and whoever will sacrifice his life for Christ's sake will find it. I need to ask you this young Kinsmor."

"I know that you would give your life for your friend, Tallow, but would you do the same for Christ? That is the question to ask." Luke returned to his workplace across the room.

Kinsmor's thoughts were already dwelling on the question before Luke asked. *How far would he go for Christ? Luke was right. He was ready to give his life in battle for a friend as a soldier of Rome, but what about sacrificing yourself for no glory? That was a hard question that would take time to answer.*

The games were the only thing mentioned in the empire at this time. Kinsmor was relieved that only the best warriors were chosen for the arena. He and others were on light guard duty around the Coliseum. Some soldiers were sprinkled in the crowd.

The crowd was great and the carnage was greater. Limbs and blood were spread all over the arena floor, and the crowd loved every moment of it.

Kinsmor's prayers were for Tallow and God's

protection over him. He prayed that his friend would come to the same relationship that he had with God. He couldn't speak with him personally, because the gladiators were kept separate from the crowd to avoid being distracted.

The "beasts" of Germania were true to their name. They were dirty, with their hair growing everywhere they wanted it to. They didn't waste time with bathing, they just dowsed themselves with water as relief from the heat.

Kinsmor watched them from a distance and thought. *"I've seen lions with less ferocity than these beasts. I guess they 'recruited' the right group for the games."*

Another observation from Kinsmor was that of the archers. They were very secretive in their daily routine, especially when Tallow was around. He saw more than one of them nudging the other and pointing in his direction. Whatever the "secret" was, everyone was tight lipped about it.

This day's events gave Kinsmor even more concern for his friend. "God protect Tallow until he surrenders to You." The quick prayer, born out of concern, also eased his sleep that night.

Chapter Twelve:
The Decision

Two days had passed since Kinsmor had breathed the prayer of concern for his friend's protection. The whole garrison was buzzing about the "games" in the arena. The soldiers were as blood thirsty as the crowd.

Kinsmor was assigned to the inside around the perimeter of the arena, in case the crowd rushed it. He recognized several archers in "village" clothes sprinkled in the crowd.

Jesters were entertaining the crowd, while children played around their parents' feet. The laughter changed to cheers as Caesar's crowd took their place above the arena. The tumult died down as the announcer took his place.

The announcer's voice echoed throughout the coliseum. "Friends, countrymen, and citizens of Rome, the matches will begin shortly. First of all, Caesar has a little exercise for your entertainment."

"Not long ago a man came through the Roman Empire speaking of love and forgiveness. He told us to love one another, which was quite a noble task. Rome does not object to loving one another. Aphrodite would applaud you for that." The crowd chuckled.

"When others said that he was king, however, he didn't deny it. Rome has no king but Caesar, and we will gladly squash any rebellion that says otherwise. We crucified that man as an example of that."

"Now there is another problem." Kinsmor's grip tightened on his sword and shield as he glared at the announcer. "The followers of this 'Christ' still preach love and forgiveness, but more treacherous is their belief in 'Christ' as their king. They have even taken his name as their own. Ladies and gentlemen…I give you…the Christians of the Roman Empire."

The crowd erupted with boos, throwing trash on those who were pushed in front of swords and spears. "Let's see if your loving God will save you now."

Kinsmor heard the lions coming. He scanned the victims in the arena, then snapped his head left and right to look for the lions.

He leaped over the wall in between a lion and its "prey". The lioness hit his shield with such force it threw him into a tumble. He quickly recovered as it charged again. The lion sunk its claws into the shield. Kinsmor lifted the beast's head and shoulders up and drove his sword deep into its torso. He heard its last moan of life as he tossed the carcass off of him.

Kinsmor saw welcomed friendly eyes as he stepped away from the lion.

Brutus and Tallow enjoyed seeing him walk their way. "I'm a bit surprised to see you here." Tallow said as Kinsmor sided with him.

"I like the odds; besides, you saved my dog." He said as he gave his friend a wink.

The carnage of the lions was dulling so the gate keepers carefully let them go through.

Tallow waved his sword to calm the cheering crowd. When the noise was down to a murmur, he started his speech. He told of his life, from the dying soldier's "question" to his present decision.

Kinsmor saw the archers throw off their beggars' clothes and make their bows ready. "God. Help me to make You proud."

At that moment he saw a toddler break into the arena. His mother lunged after him. He saw the archers draw a line on the woman and the child. He bolted toward them and swallowed them in his arms.

The arrows sunk deep into his trunk and the force of his body threw the woman and the child to the ground. They crawled out from under him unharmed.

"Greater love hath no man than this, that a man lay down his life for his friends."
--John 15:13

Authors Bio

Scott Risch grew up and currently resides in South Texas. He enjoyed the artistic side of school. Scott, enjoys lounging in the back yard and writing about the adventuress critters he observes. Scott and his wife Karyn, currently reside in Pearland, Texas. Karyn, a pre-Kindergarten teacher is an excellent source of encouragement and kid knowledge.

Other Titles by Scott Risch

Title: *Squirrel Chronicles*
- Author: Scott Risch
- Publisher: Mouse Gate Press
- Paper Back: ISBN: 9781590951231
- eBook: ISBN: 9781648835087
- Number of pages: 64
- Publication Date: 2020

Squirrel Chronicles tells the adventures of a squirrel named Smokey and his buddy Ringer. In their experiences, these two young squirrels learn life lessons, friendship, loving your enemies, and most importantly the love of the Creator.

Parents, teachers, librarians, and kids will appreciate the worldwide geography and appropriate language for Ages 6–10 Grades: 1–5.

A Journey of a Champion series:

Title: *Tallow*
A Journey of a Champion
- Author: Scott Risch
- Publisher: Mouse Gate Press
- Paper Back: ISBN: 9781648830822
- eBook: ISBN: 9781648830839
- Number of pages: 100
- Publication Date: 2021

A Roman soldier observes Tallow defending a helpless dog against the bullying boys of the village. His fighting skills intrigue the soldier. The soldier reports on the boy to his superiors and they decide to take the boy to be a soldier in the summer after his 11th year. Tallow earns the respect of his comrades and his superiors as he grows up in the Roman army. After his first battle, Tallow enters into a "quest", spawned by a dying soldier's questions. Those questions lead Tallow in pursuit of a man who can answer them. The answers to these questions are more than Tallow wants to face. His quest ends when his pride surrenders to the man. amazon.com

Title: *Brutus*
In the Shadow of Forgiveness
- Author: Scott Risch
- Publisher: Mouse Gate Press
- Paper Back: ISBN: 9781648831621
- eBook: ISBN: 9781648831638
- Number of pages: 76
- Publication Date: 2022

Brutus is a roman soldier left for dead in a martyr's arena. A woman nurses him back to health and they begin a desert journey to escape Rome.

The journey confronts Brutus with memories of his childhood that still haunt him. He is called to a decision when one of those "memories" stands before him.

Title: *Grayboe*
The Archer

- Author: Scott Risch
- Publisher: Mouse Gate Press
- Paper Back: ISBN: 9781648830822
- eBook: ISBN: 9781648830839
- Number of pages: 70
- Publication Date: 2022

Grayboe is a boy like every other boy in the Roman Empire. His skills in the hunt as an archer make him especially desirable to the Roman army. He excels above the other archers in this army.

An arrow through his bicep confronts him with a concept he hasn't heard before. Luke the physician introduces and confronts Grayboe with… "Forgiveness." Will he yield to it or build a wall against it?

Title: *Kensmore*
Courage in the Shadows
- Author: Scott Risch
- Publisher: Mouse Gate Press
- Paper Back: ISBN: 9781648833106
- eBook: ISBN: 9781648833113
- Number of pages: 60
- Publication Date: 2023

Kinsmor was a young shepherd boy who was taken by Roman solders and drafted into the Roman army.

During training in the Roman army, he became friends with Tallow, Grayboe, the doctor Luke, and was antagonized by Brutus.

Kinsmor quickly learned the skill of sward and shield. Over the years of training to be a soldier, Kinsmor gained strength and wisdom and became one of the Roman army's best.

www.ingramcontent.com/pod-product-compliance
Lightning Source LLC
Chambersburg PA
CBHW030439120726
47903CB00003B/1030